GW00481068

In loving memory of Keira Nicole, Mia and to all the babies gone too soon and the families who keep them in their hearts always. To Sebastian, Max, Florence and all the rainbow babies who bring joy after the storm.

There was once a boy called Sebastian who belonged to his Mummy and Daddy. They lived together in a lovely house, which was warm and cosy.

But, he always felt that something was missing.

He wasn't quite sure what.

Sebastian loved bubbles.

He loved how they floated on the air, lifting higher and higher with their rainbow colours shining in the sun.

His Mummy and Daddy had made him a wonderful garden to play in and one day, they put some bubble mixture into his bubble machine and left it blowing bubbles in the corner of the garden.

What Mummy and Daddy didn't know was that that corner of the garden was magic! As the bubbles came out of the machine, Sebastian found himself surrounded by lots of colourful bubbles until.....POP! He found himself INSIDE a bubble!

Sebastian couldn't quite believe it! He was inside a bubble. But he couldn't see his garden anymore....oh no! He could see a whole new world around him!

Everything was rainbow coloured –
the leaves on the trees, the flowers
and even the birds!

"Where am I ?" he wondered as he started to walk around,
kicking some rainbow coloured stones beneath his feet.

All of a sudden, he heard someone crying. It was a sad cry, small but deep and coming from behind a tree. Sebastian carefully tiptoed towards the crying noise, wondering who on earth was so sad.

It was a small white bear, with a beautiful white skirt on, sat under the tree with a book in her hand.

"Hello?" Sebastian said quietly, so not to frighten her.

The bear stopped crying and looked up to see Sebastian.

"Oh....Oh....Hello!" She answered "Who are you?

"I'm Sebastian" he replied

"Hello Sebastian, my name is Keira" she said,

wiping away a tear.

"Why are you crying?" Sebastian asked

"I am lost" the bear replied.

Sebastian thought for a moment—

"I think I am lost too!" he said.

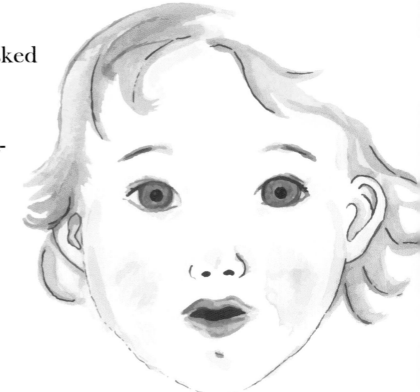

Keira got up and began to smile a little.

"Where are you from?"

"Well....I was in my garden" he explained "Then all of a sudden, I was here! Where are we?"

"This is Rainbowland" Keira replied

Sebastian took Keira's hand "Come on!"

He said " Let us see if we can find your home"

They wandered all around Rainbowland, through the meadows, across the woods and up to the beautiful Rainbow waterfalls. At each new place, Sebastian would ask "Is this it?"

Keira would shake her head each time and sigh.

"The problem is" She said "I don't even know where I am from! I don't belong anywhere!"

Sebastian was puzzled. Surely she must know where she lived!
He knew he belonged to Mummy and Daddy back in the
house with his beautiful garden.

Then he realised. He belonged to Mummy and Daddy.

Perhaps Keira needed to belong to someone too!

"Do you have a Mummy and Daddy?" he asked

"I can't remember" Keira started to feel sad again

"Well, why don't you share mine?" Sebastian suggested "You
can belong with us!"

Keira smiled a great big smile.

"I'd like that" She said "But I don't think I can come with you"

"Why not?" Sebastian asked

Keira raised the book in her hand

"It's in this book"

Keira opened the book. It was beautiful, with lovely writing inside and pictures of butterflies, hearts and flowers.

"Look here" She said, pointing to the words.

"Rainbowland is a special place,

A land between time and space,

A land in a bubble where dreams come true

But your dreams cannot leave with you,

For magic creatures cannot move or speak,

If home in another land you seek.

Only Rainbowland holds the key

For magical creatures to be free"

"What does that mean?" Sebastian asked

"It means if I leave Rainbowland I can't talk or move or anything!"

Sebastian frowned. Surely there was a way Keira could belong to his family, but not feel sad.

"I know!" he jumped up in excitement

" How about you come home with me, but every time we play in my garden, we come back to Rainbowland? If you believe you belong, you always will....with us!"

Keira seemed unsure. She wanted to run around and talk and play, but she couldn't if she went with Sebastian.

But...oh...how she longed to belong and feel loved.

"OK" she said carefully "Let's try"

Sebastian held her hand tightly and they walked to the edge of the bubble.

They were back in Sebastian's garden.

"We did it! We did it!" Sebastian cried.

But Keira said nothing. She sat on the floor, still holding Sebastian's hand.

"It's OK" He said "We can go back there tomorrow"

He took Keira up to his house to show his Mummy and
Daddy.

"Oh what a beautiful Bear!" They said, giving her a hug.

They found her a special place to sit in their house and
talked to her every day.

Although she couldn't talk back, she felt very much like
she belonged!

True to his word, Sebastian took Keira into the garden every day, and when his Mummy and Daddy put on the bubble machine...."

They were once again in Rainbowland, ready for some amazing adventures together.

LOVE

It bears all things,

believes all things,

and endures all things.

Love never ends.

How many butterflies did you spot?

Chalk Hill Blue

Clouded Yellow

Red Admiral

Essex Skipper

Duke of Burgundy

Tortoiseshall

Peacock

Clearwing

Large Heath

Small White

Dingy
Skipper

Green
Hairstreak

Adonis
Blue

Monarch

Green Veined
White

Painted
Lady

Comma

Gatekeeper

Grayling

Further reading

Sands: Neonatal and stillbirth charity- sands.org uk

Miscarriage Association: Pregnancy loss information and support - miscarriageassociation.org.uk

Bliss: For babies born premature or sick- bliss.org.uk

Child Bereavement UK: Help children and young people (up to 25), parents, and families, to rebuild their lives when a child grieves or when a child dies - childbereavementuk.org

Count The Kicks: Educating parents about the importance of tracking baby movements during the third trimester of pregnancy – countthekicks.org

ICP Support: Everything you need to know about intrahepatic cholestasis of pregnancy - icpsupport.org

Printed in Great Britain
by Amazon